© 1992 The Walt Disney Company

No portion of this book may be reproduced
without the written consent of The Walt Disney Company.

Produced by Kroha Associates, Inc.
Middletown, Connecticut

Illustrated by Yakovetic Productions

Printed in the United States of America.

ISBN 1-56326-169-3

The Magic Melody

Deep beneath the sea, in a cavern at the bottom of the ocean, the evil sea witch Ursula gazed into her magic pearl. There she saw the Little Mermaid admiring her father's shiny gold trident. "If only *I* had the king's trident," she growled, "things would be different around here!"

There was nothing Ursula wanted more than to be queen of the undersea kingdom, but she needed the king's trident to do it. The trident contained great power, and whoever held it could have any wish he desired.

That is why King Triton never let anyone else even touch the trident — except, of course, for his lovely daughter, Ariel.

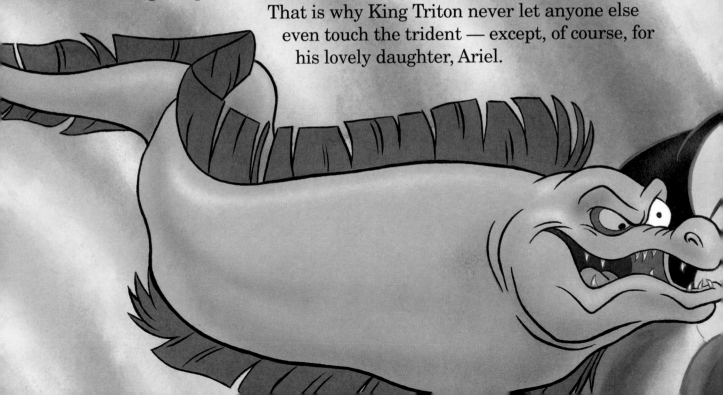

"I've got an idea!" Ursula cackled gleefully. "I will trick Ariel into giving the trident to me!"

"How will you do that?" hissed the eels, Flotsam and Jetsam.

"Everyone knows how much the Little Mermaid loves getting presents," the sea witch explained. "Well, I have a very *special* present for her."

Ursula dug down deep into her bag of tricks and pulled out a gaily wrapped package. She and her eels swam to the entrance of Ariel's grotto and left the present outside, where the Little Mermaid would be sure to find it.

"A present!" Ariel cried when she discovered the box. "I wonder who it could be from?"

"Open it and find out!" replied Flounder excitedly.

The Little Mermaid quickly tore off the ribbon and paper and opened the package. Inside was a beautiful silver music box decorated with tiny gold instruments and musical notes. There was also a letter which read, *Play this music box before you go to bed. The soothing melody will lull you into a sleep filled with sweet dreams.*

"Oh, how thoughtful!" exclaimed Ariel. "Maybe it's from Sebastian. He knows how much I love music!"

Later that same day, as Sebastian the crab was making his way to Ariel's grotto for a visit, he heard Ursula's evil laugh drifting out of her lair. Knowing the witch must be up to no good, he crept closer and listened as Ursula explained the rest of her plan to the eels. "When Ariel hears the melody from the music box three times, she will fall into a trance," Ursula said with glee. "Once she is under my spell, she will steal her father's trident and bring it here to me. Then I will rule the sea!"

This is terrible! Sebastian thought. *I must stop Ariel before it's too late!*

Ariel couldn't wait for bedtime to listen to the music box. She opened the lid and listened as the soft, sweet melody floated out. The gentle, soothing harmonies of harps and flutes and violins filled her head with the most delightful music she had ever heard. She listened to it a second time. The delicate notes dancing in her head made her start to feel sleepy. Then, just as she was about to listen to the melody for the *third* time…

Sebastian came charging into the grotto. "Stop!" he cried, slamming the music box shut to stop the melody. "Don't listen to that music! It's one of Ursula's spells!" Sebastian explained how he had overheard Ursula's plan to trick Ariel into stealing her father's trident.

"Ursula — queen of the sea? It's too horrible to even think about!" Ariel said angrily. "But now what do we do? If I don't bring her my father's trident, then she'll know the spell didn't work."

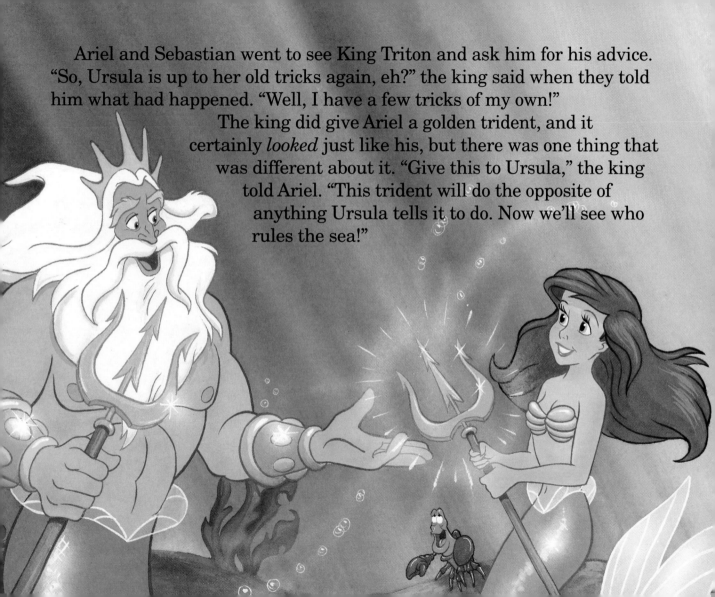

Ariel and Sebastian went to see King Triton and ask him for his advice. "So, Ursula is up to her old tricks again, eh?" the king said when they told him what had happened. "Well, I have a few tricks of my own!"

The king did give Ariel a golden trident, and it certainly *looked* just like his, but there was one thing that was different about it. "Give this to Ursula," the king told Ariel. "This trident will do the opposite of anything Ursula tells it to do. Now we'll see who rules the sea!"

Ariel was afraid the sea witch might know it was a trick, so she pretended to be under the spell of the magic melody. As she slowly floated past the sea witch she held the fake trident out to her. "As you have commanded," she said, her heart pounding.

"At last!" Ursula screeched, snatching the trident from Ariel's hands. "King Triton's power now belongs to me! Anything I wish for will be mine!"

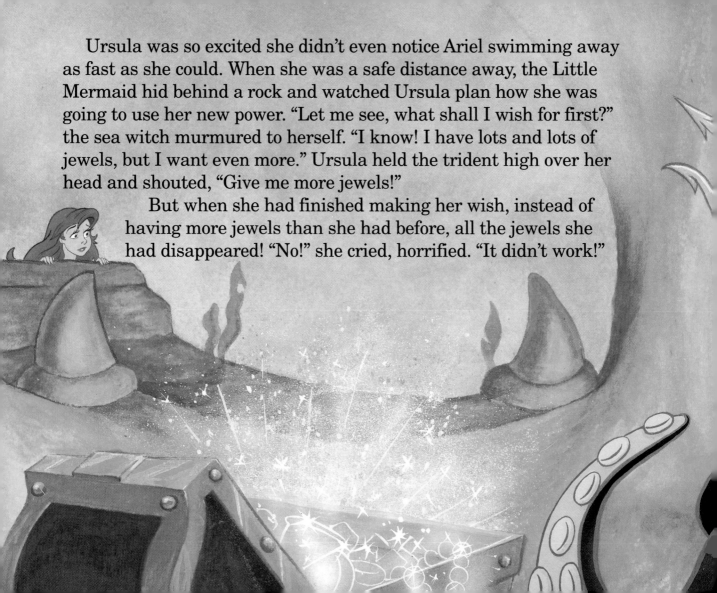

Ursula was so excited she didn't even notice Ariel swimming away as fast as she could. When she was a safe distance away, the Little Mermaid hid behind a rock and watched Ursula plan how she was going to use her new power. "Let me see, what shall I wish for first?" the sea witch murmured to herself. "I know! I have lots and lots of jewels, but I want even more." Ursula held the trident high over her head and shouted, "Give me more jewels!"

But when she had finished making her wish, instead of having more jewels than she had before, all the jewels she had disappeared! "No!" she cried, horrified. "It didn't work!"

Several sea horses had gathered to see what was going on. Ursula hated sea horses. They were always so playful and happy. "Go away!" she yelled. But the curious creatures stayed right where they were. "I said go away!" she shouted again. And then, remembering she had the king's trident, she held it high above her head and said, "I command you to go away. It is my wish!"

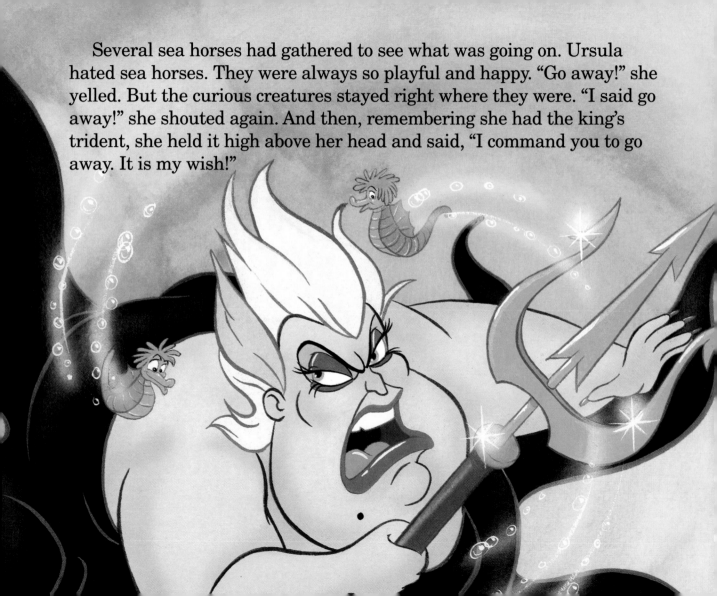

But instead of going away as she had commanded, the sea horses came even closer! And soon they were joined by even more sea horses who perched themselves all along the sea witch's outstretched tentacles! Now Ursula knew that something was wrong. "I've been tricked!" she howled, whirling around in a circle to shake off the creatures.

"I wish I'd never seen this horrible trident!" Ursula shouted. Suddenly her lair was filled with heavy gold tridents. Once again the trident had granted her the *opposite* of what she'd wished for. In a rage, Ursula broke the magic trident in two.

The next morning, Ariel returned to Ursula's lair and gave her back the music box. "Sebastian told me you left this gift for me outside the grotto," she said. "It was really very sweet of you, and I do appreciate the thought, but I'm afraid I can't accept it. My father won't allow it."

Ursula was very upset. She wasn't sure why the trident hadn't worked, but she knew that Ariel must have had something to do with it. "Someday," she muttered to herself as Ariel swam away, "I'm going to get that mermaid."

When Ariel told her father what had happened when Ursula made her wishes, the king laughed so hard he almost couldn't stop. "I wish I could have seen that!" he said when he finally caught his breath.

"But what will we do if she tries to get your trident again?" Ariel asked.

"Oh, I wouldn't worry about that," replied Sebastian. "Ursula's greedy ways always seem to get the best of her — one way or the other!"